Jack Frost's
Ice Castle
Animal Shelter
CHILDREN'S HOSPITAL
Village
Hall
Children's
Hospital

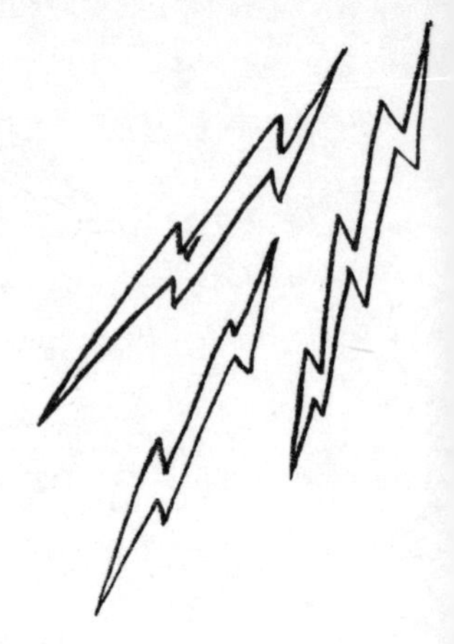

Jack Frost's Spell

Give me candy! Give me sweets!
Give me sticky, fizzy treats!
Lollipops and fudge so yummy -
Bring them here to fill my tummy.

Monica, I'll steal from you.
Gabby, Lisa, Shelley too.
I will build a sweetie shop,
So I can eat until I pop!

Contents

The Playground Buddy

Rachel Walker whizzed down the candy-cane slide. She squealed with laughter as she zoomed off the end on to a trampoline and bounced into the air.

"This is the best park in the whole wide world," she called happily to her best friend, Kirsty Tate, who was sitting at the top of the slide.

"WHEEEEEE!" Kirsty sang out as she shot down the slide and bounced down beside Rachel. "It's so much fun. I'm so glad that Aunt Harri asked us both to meet her here."

Rachel was staying with Kirsty for a whole week. It was always fun visiting Wetherbury, but this time it was extra exciting. Kirsty's Aunt Harri, who worked at the Candy Land sweet factory, had asked the girls to help her with some very special deliveries. Candy Land was giving out Helping Hands awards for people who were doing wonderful things to help the community. It was part of Aunt Harri's job to present the winners with bags of their favourite sweets, and Rachel and Kirsty were proud to help.

"I expect your Aunt Harri will be here soon," said Rachel, checking her watch.

The girls stopped bouncing and looked over at the factory. The sweet-themed park was in the beautiful grounds of the factory, on the outskirts of Wetherbury.

The tall slide looked as if it had been made from candy canes, the swings were shaped like jelly beans and the roundabout looked like a circle of liquorice. On the far side of the park, some boys were playing by a fence that seemed to be made of strawberry laces.

Just then, Kirsty noticed a little boy sitting on one end of the seesaw, which was shaped like a stick of rock.

"That little boy looks sad," she said. "I wonder if he is lonely. Maybe one of us should go and sit on the other end of the seesaw so he can have a turn."

"I think someone else has already had that idea," said Rachel.

A girl with long brown hair was walking towards the seesaw, smiling. She

said something to the little boy, and a smile lit up his face. Then she sat on the other end of the seesaw and started to go up and down.

"What a kind girl," said Kirsty. "I noticed her earlier, pushing a little girl on the swings."

When the little boy's mum called him away, the girl left the seesaw and walked towards Rachel and Kirsty.

"Hi," she said in a friendly voice. "I haven't seen you here before. I'm Olivia. I'm the playground buddy for this park."

"I'm Rachel and this

is Kirsty," said Rachel. "I've never heard of a playground buddy before."

"I look out for anyone who seems lonely or on their own, and I make sure that they have someone to play with," Olivia explained. "Sometimes people make new friends here. It's so great."

"What a kind idea," said Rachel with a smile. "What made you think of it?"

"When I moved to Wetherbury, I missed my old school and my old friends," said Olivia. "I remember how it felt to be lonely and have no one to play with. I want to make sure that no one else feels like that. So I play with children who are alone, and I help them to meet new friends."

"It sounds as if you're not lonely any more either," said Kirsty.

"Definitely not," Olivia said, laughing.

"I always have friends to play with now that I'm a playground buddy."

"Every park should have one," said Rachel, with a smile.

"It's not working very well today, though," said Olivia, glancing towards the

boys by the strawberry-lace fence. "Those boys over there have driven most of the children away."

Surprise Under the Slide

The boys were all wearing matching caps, and they were blowing enormous green bubbles with their bubble gum.

"What have they been doing?" asked Kirsty.

"They've said rude things to all the children, and they've been sticking their bubble gum everywhere and making it

messy," Olivia explained. "No one wants to sit on a swing that's covered in chewed bubble gum."

She reached into her pocket and pulled out a packet of bubble gum.

"Would you like some?" she said. "I adore bubble gum, but I always put it in the bin when I've finished chewing. It makes me feel sad to see those boys spoil the playground. They're being so naughty."

Thanking her, Rachel and Kirsty each took a piece of the bright-pink bubble gum. Rachel popped hers in her mouth, but it was so hard that she couldn't chew it. She could see that Kirsty and Olivia were having the same problem. They took the gum out and dropped it into the nearby bin.

"What could be wrong?" asked Olivia in a disappointed voice. "I had a piece earlier and it was fine."

Just then, the gate of the park squeaked and a little girl came in.

"I'll go and see if she wants someone to play with," said Olivia. "It was nice to meet you both, Rachel and Kirsty. See

you later."

She walked towards the little girl, and Rachel turned to Kirsty.

"Shall we have another go on the slide?" she asked. "Oh!"

The space underneath the slide was glowing with a pink light, and both Rachel and Kirsty knew exactly what that meant. Magic! They had shared enough adventures with their friends the fairies to know when another adventure was about to arrive.

The girls ducked under the slide and smiled. Gabby the Bubble Gum Fairy was fluttering in the shadow of the slide. She floated down and hovered in front of them. Her pink hair bounced on her shoulders, and her peach-coloured skirt shimmied in the light breeze.

"Hello, Rachel and Kirsty," she said in a sweet voice. "I'm glad I found you. Will you help me to get my magical bubble gum back from Jack Frost and his goblins?"

"Of course we will," said Kirsty at once. "We had so much fun helping Monica yesterday."

"She told me how wonderful you were," said Gabby. "I'm sure I can get my magical bubble gum back if I have

your help. I need it to make sure that all bubble gum is chewy and bubblicious."

The day before, Monica the Marshmallow Fairy had whisked Rachel and Kirsty to the Sweet Factory, a special place in Fairyland where sweets grew on trees. The Candy Land Fairies – and their friends, the Sweet Fairies – were getting ready for the annual Candy Harvest. The trees were full of all kinds of delicious sweets. But as the fairies were telling the girls about the Fairyland Harvest Feast, Jack Frost and his mischievous goblins had appeared. Before anyone could stop them, they had stolen the magical sweets that belonged to the Candy Land Fairies.

"We'll do everything we can to find your magical object," said Rachel. "We just tried some bubble gum and it was

too hard to chew."

Gabby nodded.

"Without my magical sweet, I can't make sure that bubble gum is chewy and

delicious," she said. "And it's not just me. With the Harvest Feast coming up, time is running out. If we don't find the three missing magical sweets, the Harvest Feast

at the Sweet Factory will be ruined."

"Then there's no time to lose," said Kirsty. "We need to begin the search at once, and I think I know exactly where to start."

Goblin Gum

Kirsty turned to Rachel, bursting to explain her idea.

"Do you remember Olivia talking about the boys by the fence on the far side of the park?" she asked Rachel. "She said that they were blowing big bubbles with green bubble gum. But we couldn't even chew our gum, so why is their gum

making such perfect bubbles? What if they are somehow using Gabby's magic? I think they might be goblins."

"Oh my goodness," said Gabby, her eyes wide. "Do you really think that my magical bubble gum could be right here?"

"Let's find out," said Rachel.

She came out from under the slide and peered across the park towards the fence. Kirsty came to stand beside her.

"It's hard to tell," said Kirsty. "They are all wearing caps so we can't see if they have green heads."

"Look at their feet," said Rachel. "Goblins have enormous feet, and that's one thing they can't disguise."

The three boys were wearing lime-green high-top trainers, and Rachel and

Kirsty exchanged a knowing look. The trainers were enormous.

"They must be goblins," said Gabby, settling down on Rachel's shoulder. "But how can we get closer? They'll run off as soon as they see us."

"I've got an idea," said Rachel. "Gabby, can you disguise us as goblins? They won't run away if they think we're just

like them. When we're close enough, we can put the plan into action. Goblins always like a competition, and we're going to give them one."

Gabby nodded, and the girls ducked back under the slide. She waved her wand, and a tickly feeling started in the girls' hands and spread all over their bodies. They watched each other, giggling as their skin turned green. Rachel saw Kirsty's nose bubble with warts and her ears grow larger. Kirsty giggled as Rachel's feet grew twice as large, and her knees became knobbly.

There was a final bright flash of light, and then Rachel and Kirsty were no longer girls. They were dressed in skinny jeans, t-shirts and lime-green high-top trainers. Under their caps, their heads

were bald and knobbly.

"No one would guess that you're Kirsty Tate," said Rachel with a laugh. "I just hope that your Aunt Harri doesn't come looking for us early."

Kirsty smiled, and held open her pocket so that Gabby could slip inside.

"Let's go," she said.

They headed across the park towards the fence. On the way they passed Olivia, who was still playing with the little girl they had seen earlier.

"Hi, Olivia," called Kirsty, forgetting for a moment that she didn't look like herself any more.

Olivia looked a bit confused, but waved to her.

"Whoops," said Kirsty, putting her hand over her mouth. "I must remember that I'm in disguise."

The girls strolled over to the goblins, trying not to look too interested. The

goblins were still blowing bubbles. Rachel waited until the bubble that the tallest goblin was blowing went *POP*, and then laughed.

"I can blow a bigger bubble than that," she said in a boastful voice. "I can blow a

bigger bubble than anyone else here."

"Oh no you can't," said the tallest goblin.

He started to blow another bubble, and so did all the other goblins. Rachel and Kirsty watched as bubbles popped and splatted all over the goblins' faces.

"Kirsty, look," whispered Rachel.

She nodded her head in the direction of the bench. A goblin with droopy ears was sitting there, blowing a truly huge bubble. When the bubble burst, he held out his hand and squeezed his eyes shut, muttering something. Then a rectangle of green bubble gum appeared in his hand. He popped it into his mouth and chewed

it noisily. Then he started to blow an even bigger bubble than before.

"Goblins can't do their own magic," Kirsty whispered in Rachel's large green ear. "He must have Gabby's magical bubble gum!"

Code Pink Emergency

Rachel went over to where the droopy-eared goblin was sitting and bent down to speak to him.

"May I have some gum, please?" she asked politely. "I want to prove to everyone that I can blow the biggest bubbles."

The goblin looked at her in surprise.

"But of course," he said in a sing-song voice. "How do you do, and please and thank you as well."

He lifted his cap and pulled out a huge, chewed-up wad.

"Have some of this ABC gum," he said. "I've been keeping it especially for extra-polite goblins who mind their manners."

"What's ABC gum?" Rachel asked, surprised that he was being so nice.

"Already Been Chewed!" yelled the goblin, cackling with horrible laughter.

Rachel's heart sank.

"No, thanks," she said, and hurried quickly back to Kirsty.

"My idea didn't work," she said sadly. "I was too polite, and he laughed at me. Your turn, Kirsty."

"I've got a plan," said Kirsty. "I think! Wish me luck."

"Good luck," said Rachel, crossing her fingers and smiling at her friend.

Kirsty walked up to the goblin and

took a deep breath. Rachel had tried being polite, and it hadn't worked. She was going to have to be as rude as the goblins if she wanted to get the magical gum back.

"Hey, you," she said in a squawky voice. "Give me some fresh gum right now, mouldy breath. I want to blow a

giant bubble, and I want to do it now!"

The goblin scowled at her, but reached one bony hand into his pocket and pulled out a pink rectangle of sparkling bubble gum. A deliciously sweet smell filled the air. At once, Gabby zoomed out of Kirsty's pocket and swooped towards the goblin's hand.

"Look out!" shrieked a goblin from behind Kirsty. "It's a fairy!"

The droopy-eared goblin's bony fingers closed around the gum. Then a large lime-green trainer stepped between

Rachel and Kirsty, and bony elbows shoved them aside. A goblin with extra-big feet blew a massive bubble, and Gabby could not get out of the way quickly enough. She was trapped.

As Gabby tried to push her way out of the sticky bubble, the goblin roared with laughter. He stuck the bubble to the park fence and then scampered off towards the Candy Land factory, followed by all the other goblins.

"Quickly, we have to go after them," Gabby called out.

Rachel unstuck the bubble from the fence, and Kirsty poked her finger into it. With a loud *POP*, Gabby was free.

"Thank you for rescuing me," she said.

"It was horrible to feel trapped."

"Can you turn us into fairies?" Kirsty asked. "We'll be able to follow the goblins more quickly if we can fly."

Olivia and the little girl were not looking their way. Gabby waved her wand, and – *POP! POP!* – Rachel and Kirsty were goblins no longer. Now they were fluttering beside Gabby, their wings glimmering in the sunlight. They zoomed towards the factory side by side and slipped in through an open window.

The fairies were in a long corridor, with many doors set into it. They looked both ways, but the corridor was empty.

"The goblins have disappeared," said Kirsty. "Where would they have gone?"

"Shall we split up and search for them?" Gabby suggested.

"Wait," said Rachel suddenly. "There are signs on these doors. Look – each one leads to a different department."

They flew along the corridor, checking each door sign.

"*Humbug Department*," Kirsty read out loud. "*Fizzy Sweets Department. Chocolate*

Department. Marshmallow Department."

"*Bubble Gum Department*!" said Gabby with a squeak of excitement. "I bet they're in here."

The door was shut, but the gap

underneath it was big enough for a fairy to slip through.

"Out of the way!" Rachel cried, as a man's heavy feet hurried towards them.

The fairies dived sideways and flew on to a high shelf. From here, they could see that the Bubble Gum Department was in chaos. Workers in pink overalls were dashing left and right in a panic. There was an open door in the far corner of the room, labelled *Gum Testing*. More workers were staggering out, their lips stuck together with gum. A lady in a bubble-gum pink

suit was yelling into her phone.

"This is a Code Pink Emergency," she cried. "The gum has gone extra sticky. The gum testers are down. I repeat, the

gum testers are down."

She listened for a moment and then put down the phone.

"Evacuate the Bubble Gum Department!" she yelled to the other workers. "Everyone out!"

The workers stampeded out of the department, and Rachel grabbed Kirsty and Gabby by the hands.

"The goblins are behind this," she said. "Come on, we have to go in."

A Barrel of Gum

The fairies flew into the testing room. They saw little tables filled with brightly coloured bubble gum, comfortable chairs and plenty of whiteboards where testers could write notes about the gum. But there were no goblins.

"Over there," said Kirsty, spotting another open door.

The sign on the door said *Gum-Making Room*. As they flew towards it, Rachel spotted one of the Candy Land Helping Hands bags on a table. It was filled with bubble gum, and it had Olivia's name on it.

"Oh no," Rachel said with a groan. "Olivia's going to win a prize, but it won't be any good unless we can get the magical bubble gum back."

"Don't worry," said Kirsty in a

determined voice. "That's exactly what we're going to do."

They flew through the doorway into a noisy warehouse filled with clanking, hissing machines. A maze of conveyor belts circled the room. Some carried piles of bubble gum and tipped it into chutes, which led to packaging machines. Others carried packets of bubble gum to large

Candy Land boxes.

The goblins were capering on one of the conveyor belts, trampling on the gum. The droopy-eared goblin was throwing handfuls of bubble gum around like confetti. Another was kicking it into the air. They were cackling and squawking with the fun of mischief.

"We have to stop them," said Gabby with a groan. "They're going to spoil all the bubble gum unless I can get my magical sweet back."

Suddenly, Kirsty noticed a big barrel of warm bubble gum mixture standing near one of the conveyor belts. The thick, sticky goo was waiting to be cooled and shaped into rectangles.

"Gabby, I've got an idea," she said. "Can you use your magic to move that barrel and reverse the conveyor belt?"

Gabby's eyes twinkled when she understood Kirsty's plan, and she nodded. Her wand flicked up and down like a conductor's baton, and then the barrel began to scrape across the floor. The bubble gum goo sloshed as the barrel bumped against the end of the conveyor belt. Then Gabby tapped her wand against the side of the conveyor belt, and it juddered to a stop.

"What's wrong with it?" squawked the droopy-eared goblin. "Stupid thing."

CLANK! The machinery went into reverse, and the conveyor belt sent the goblins whizzing back towards the barrel. One after another, they plopped into the pink mixture. They wriggled and jiggled, but it was no use. They were well and truly stuck.

"I can't move!" wailed the droopy-eared goblin.

"Get me out of here!" shouted another.

Rachel, Kirsty and Gabby fluttered over to the barrel and perched on the rim.

"Gabby will get you out," said Kirsty, "but only after you return her magical bubble gum."

"No way," the goblins grumbled. "We're not doing anything you say, silly fairies."

They tried clambering over each other to get out, and they tried pushing each other out. Nothing worked. The fairies simply waited and watched. Eventually, the goblins started to whisper to each other. At first some of them shook their heads, but eventually they were all nodding. Every single one of them looked miserable.

"Jack Frost's going to go purple," the smallest goblin muttered. "I don't like it when he gets cross."

"Well, I don't like being stuck in a barrel," said the goblin with the droopy ears. "The fun's over."

He managed to squirm through the goo, and held his hand up in the air. He was holding Gabby's magic bubble gum.

A smile lit up Gabby's face as she took

the bubble gum in her delicate fingers. It shrank to fairy size at once, and she waved her wand and spoke the words of a spell.

"*Return these goblins to the floor.*

They won't cause trouble any more.

Clean them up and give them gum,

To keep them all from feeling glum."

The goblins found themselves standing beside the barrel, as clean as before they fell in. Each of them was holding a packet of bubble gum. Big grins started

to spread across all of their faces.

"Come on, let's go back to the playground," said the goblin with droopy ears. "I'll show you the biggest bubble ever."

"Rubbish," the smallest goblin retorted. "Your bubble will look like a wrinkly raisin compared to mine. I'm the best, and my bubble will be, too."

Squabbling loudly, the goblins ran out of the room.

Big Bubbles

Gabby waved her wand again, and at once the room was sparkling clean. In fact, it looked better than it had before. The barrel was back in its place and the bubble gum was travelling neatly along the conveyor belts. There was no sign that the goblins had ever been there.

Gabby hugged Rachel and Kirsty, and

then gently tapped their shoulders with her wand. They returned to their normal size in the blink of an eye.

Just then, they heard a sound that grew

louder and louder.

"It's footsteps," said Rachel in alarm. "Someone's coming."

Gabby slipped into Rachel's pocket, just

as the factory workers came back into the room, following the lady in the pink suit. Everyone looked a lot happier.

"I'm delighted that all the gum testers' mouths have been unstuck," the lady said. "Everything seems to be back to normal

in here, so please return to your work."

Pressing themselves back against the wall, Rachel and Kirsty edged around the room and out of the door. They had just reached the Helping Hands bag of bubble gum when they heard a familiar voice.

"Girls? What a surprise to see you in here!"

It was Aunt Harri. She came over to them, smiling.

"I see you've found the next Helping Hands prize," she said. "The winner is a girl

called Olivia, who has been a wonderful playground buddy in our Candy Land playground. Would you like to come and present the prize with me right now?"

The girls agreed eagerly, relieved that

Aunt Harri hadn't asked them to explain what they were doing in the Bubble Gum Department. Soon they were heading towards the playground. More children had arrived, and the goblins were there

too. Aunt Harri called Olivia over to her and everyone gathered around.

"Olivia, the other children who use this playground think that you are a very kind person," said Aunt Harri. "They have voted for you to be the winner of today's Helping Hands award. We hope that you enjoy your prize."

Olivia's eyes filled with surprised, happy tears as Rachel and Kirsty gave her the bag of bubble gum. Everyone burst into applause.

"Thank you all," Olivia said, gazing around at the friendly, smiling faces. "I hope you'll share it with me."

She shared out the bubble gum, and soon everyone was blowing big, beautiful bubbles – even Aunt Harri!

"This gum is deliciously soft and

chewy," said Kirsty. "I'm so happy."

"The goblins are happy, too," said Rachel, with a smile.

The goblins were joining in with the bubble-blowing, and even clapped when Olivia managed to blow the biggest

bubble of all. While everyone else was laughing and playing, Rachel and Kirsty ducked under the slide. Gabby fluttered out of Rachel's pocket and gave each of

them a gentle kiss on the cheek.

"Thank you for helping me today," she said. "We are one step closer to making the Harvest Feast a success."

"Please tell Lisa and Shelley that we'll

be ready to help find the other missing sweets," Kirsty said, looking determined.

Gabby blew a fairy-sized bubble. Its colour changed and shimmered from pink to lilac to purple and back to pink again. It was the tiniest, most perfect bubble that the girls had ever seen. As they gazed at it,

Gabby disappeared with a *POP*. She had gone back to Fairyland, but her bubble drifted upwards, higher and higher into the sky.

"Do you think that we'll be able to find the other two magical objects for the Candy Land Fairies before the Harvest Feast?" Kirsty asked her best friend.

Rachel nodded.

"Definitely. We won't let Jack Frost spoil things for the fairies," she said. "But right now, I want another go on this amazing slide. Race you!"

The End

Now it's time for Kirsty and Rachel to help ...

Lisa the Jelly Bean Fairy

Read on for a sneak peek ...

"This is a bumpy ride!" said Kirsty Tate with a laugh.

She and her best friend Rachel Walker giggled as they bounced up and down. Kirsty's Aunt Harri patted the dashboard.

"I love this good old Candy Land van," she said. "Even if it is a bit noisy and bumpy."

Candy Land was the sweet factory just outside the village, and Aunt Harri was lucky enough to work there.

"Candy Land is my second favourite thing about Wetherbury," said Rachel.

"What's your favourite?" asked Kirsty.

"Staying with you, of course," said Rachel with a grin. "It's always magical."

Rachel had come to visit Kirsty for the school holidays. Ever since they had become best friends, they had also been good friends with the fairies. Magic always seemed to follow them around when they were together. Sometimes they thought that it was as if their friendship cast a very special spell.

This time, Monica the Marshmallow Fairy had whisked them away to the Fairyland Sweet Factory, where sweets grew on trees. They had met the other Candy Land Fairies, who used their magical objects to make sure that all candy was sweet and delicious. They were getting ready for the annual Harvest Feast, and asked Rachel and Kirsty if they would like to come. But just then,

Jack Frost had appeared with his goblins. He had stolen the Candy Land fairies' magical objects so that he could keep all sweets for himself.

Kirsty and Rachel had helped two of the Candy Land Fairies to get their magical objects back, but there were still two more to find. However, today they had something else on their minds. They were on their way to see a boy called Tal, who volunteered as a dog walker at the Wetherbury Animal Shelter.

"I can't wait to see Tal's face when he finds out that he's a winner," said Kirsty.

Candy Land had been giving its Helping Hands Awards to young people who did helpful things in the community. The girls had been helping Aunt Harri to surprise the winners with special bags of Candy Land treats.

"What's inside Tal's Candy Land bag?" Rachel asked.

"Jelly beans," said Aunt Harri, smiling.

"Yum, I love jelly beans," said Kirsty.

"I brought along a small packet of them for you to share," said Aunt Harri. "You'll find them in the back of my seat."

Rachel put her hand into the little pocket on the back of Aunt Harri's seat, and found the packet. She opened it and chose a purple one.

Calling all parents, carers and teachers!
The Rainbow Magic fairies are here to help your child enter the magical world of reading. Whatever reading stage they are at, there's a Rainbow Magic book for everyone! Here is Lydia the Reading Fairy's guide to supporting your child's journey at all levels.

1

Starting Out

Our Rainbow Magic Beginner Readers are perfect for first-time readers who are just beginning to develop reading skills and confidence. Approved by teachers, they contain a full range of educational levelling, as well as lively full-colour illustrations.

2

Developing Readers

Rainbow Magic Early Readers contain longer stories and wider vocabulary for building stamina and growing confidence. These are adaptations of our most popular Rainbow Magic stories, specially developed for younger readers in conjunction with an Early Years reading consultant, with full-colour illustrations.

3

Going Solo

The Rainbow Magic chapter books – a mixture of series and one-off specials – contain accessible writing to encourage your child to venture into reading independently. These highly collectible and much-loved magical stories inspire a love of reading to last a lifetime.

www.rainbowmagicbooks.co.uk

"Rainbow Magic got my daughter reading chapter books. Great sparkly covers, cute fairies and traditional stories full of magic that she found impossible to put down" – Mother of Edie (6 years)

"Florence LOVES the Rainbow Magic books. She really enjoys reading now" – Mother of Florence (6 years)

The Rainbow Magic Reading Challenge

Well done, fairy friend – you have completed the book!
This book was worth 10 points.

See how far you have climbed on the
Reading Rainbow opposite.

The more books you read, the more points you will get, and the closer you will be to becoming a Fairy Princess!

Do you want your own Reading Rainbow?

1. Cut out the coin below
2. Go to the Rainbow Magic website
3. Download and print out your poster
4. Add your coin and climb up the Reading Rainbow!

There's all this and lots more at
www.rainbowmagicbooks.co.uk

You'll find activities, competitions, stories, a special newsletter and complete profiles of all the Rainbow Magic fairies. Find a fairy with your name!